WHAT COLOR IS YOUR DRAGON?

Contact: Facebook/Cynthia Star books @cynthiastarbooks

"What color is your dragon?" Joe asked me one day.

"What? I don't have a dragon."

"Everyone has a dragon."

"That would be fun. Too bad
they aren't REAL."

"Of course, they are! My dragon is green. He's a lean, green, flying machine. He's got gold wings, and the tip of his tail glows. He's soooo cool!"

"And I suppose you RIDE your dragon?" I asked.

"He's the fastest dragon around!"

"There are *more* dragons?"

"They're everywhere.
I told you, EVERYONE
has a dragon.
But not everyone
can see them."

"Wait! Can you teach ME to see dragons?"

"You can't see dragons unless you believe they're real."

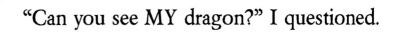

"Can you see MY dragon?" I questioned.

"Nope, not until you find him yourself."

That night I got out all my books about dragons and started to read.

I fell asleep, hoping to dream of my dragon.

But he wasn't there.

When I woke up, all I could think of was dragons.

So I got up and started to look.

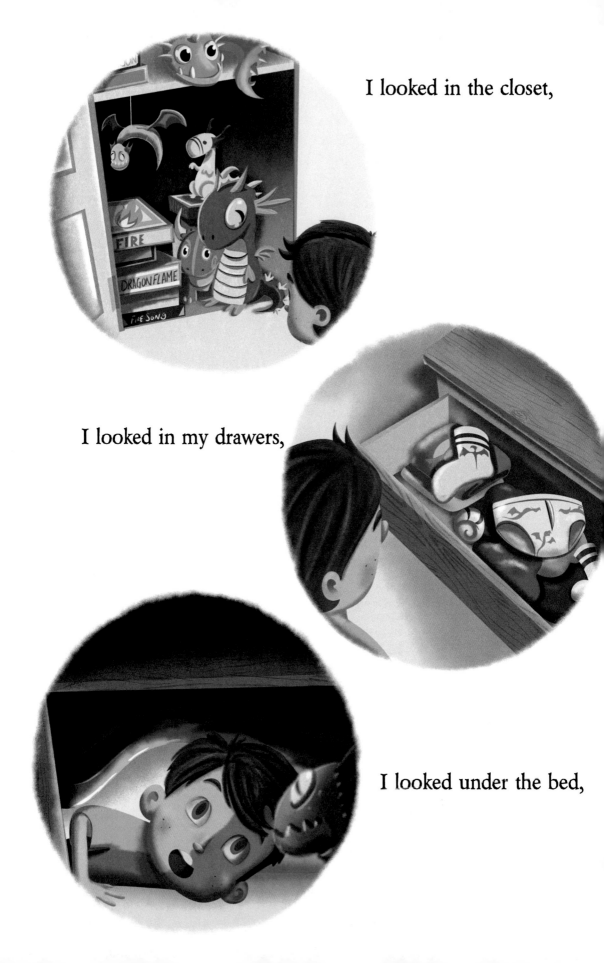

I looked in the closet,

I looked in my drawers,

I looked under the bed,

and under the chairs.

I looked in the
bathroom,

I looked down the stairs,

I looked behind trees,

and under the fence.

I even looked in the garbage

and down the street.

But he wasn't there.

"This isn't fair."

"Does everyone else have a dragon but me?"

"Why can't I see my dragon?
Where is he?"

"If I was a dragon, where would I be?"

At first, I didn't see anything,
but I kept thinking about my dragon.

What color would he be?
How big is he?
"Where, oh! Where is he?"

And then...

I saw the outline of the biggest dragon's head I had ever seen! It moved, and I caught a glimpse of wings on his back as they started to unfold.

"Oh, WOW!" The wings
were so big that they took up
an entire cloud.

His neck was bowed, and he was
the bluest, blue I ever saw. Silver
scales glistened beneath his wings,
and he shone so bright, I had to
shield my eyes!

He flapped his wings and began to fly away.
"What? You're leaving already? Wait, you can't go!"

I jumped up and waved to the dragon. "Hello, dragon! I see you!"
But he kept on flying in the other direction.

"Look over here, dragon. Come back dragon!"

I kept yelling, waving, and calling to the dragon.
Soon, he was entirely out of sight.

"Noooooo....," I wailed. "This can't be."

I finally see a dragon, and he just...flies away?
What if I never see another dragon again? What if... wait a minute.
What if that was MY dragon? And I let him go!

I leaped to my feet and started yelling and screaming.

"You're my dragon!
I know you are.
Come back!
Come back, my dragon!"

I yelled again, "You're
my dragon! Come
back, my dragon!"

"Please come back," I whispered.
I kept looking at the spot where I last saw him. Then I saw a tiny speck, way out in the distance.

Was that my dragon?

Was he coming back?

Yes, that's him!

I could tell he was
descending at a rapid speed,
faster and faster…headed
straight towards me.

The swish of his wings filled my head.

Swoosh, swoosh!

I laughed as I covered my ears.

My dragon was REAL!

He landed with a soft thump and stood in front of me with wings folded at his sides.

"Hi dragon, I'm David. I've been looking for you. Will you be my dragon?"

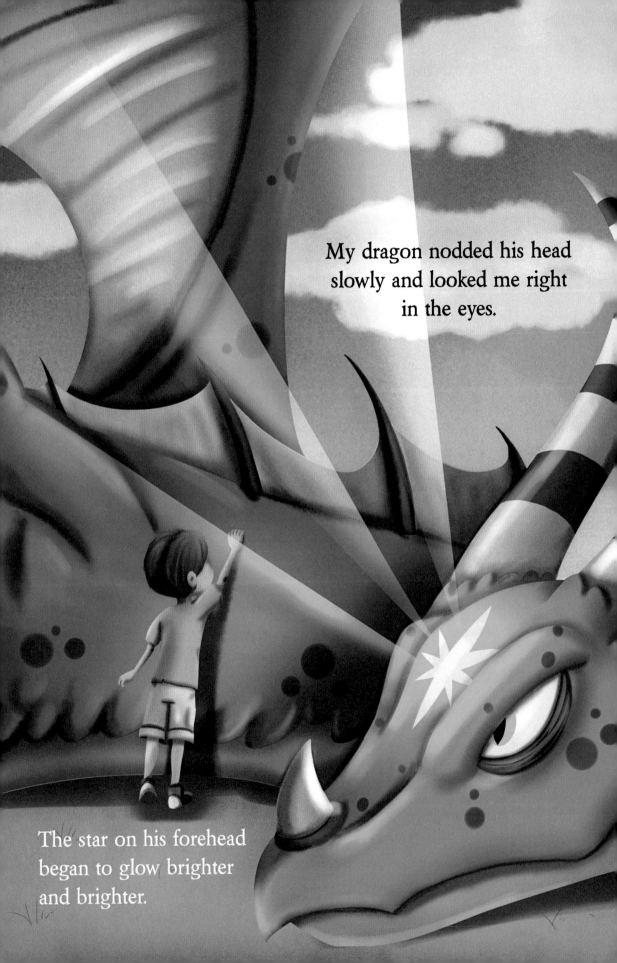

My dragon nodded his head slowly and looked me right in the eyes.

The star on his forehead began to glow brighter and brighter.

Joe and I race our dragons, and now, I can see other dragons, all over the place.

But I was wondering...

"What color is YOUR dragon?"

Made in the USA
Las Vegas, NV
12 December 2024

14013036R00021